THE MYSTERIOUS LAB

AAKASH DAVE

Made with ♥ on the Notion Press Platform
www.notionpress.com

I have dedicated this book to my father . Due to him I have been able to reach this far . He has been with me througout my journey and has shown great enthusiasm towards my story . I am very grateful to him .

Contents

1. Introduction   1

2. Who Could It Be ?   2

3. James And David   4

4. One More Case   5

5. Are We Lost !   6

6. Did You Hear That   8

7. 4 Investigators   9

8. The Search Begins   10

9. What ! How Did This Happen ?   11

10. Why What When How ?   12

11. The Stratergy   13

12. Plan In Action   14

13. The Truth   15

14. A Giant Giant Robot   18

15. Room To Room   20

16. What's The Password ?   22

17. The Antidode   23

18. Trump Card   24

19. Back Home   25

Introduction

Once upon a time there was a nice and peaceful town. children went to school, men and women went to jobs and everyone was happy. but one day something happened. something terrible. One Halloween night everybody had a good time and then went home. It was 2AM. a poor beggar was walking on the street. suddenly everybody woke up. everybody in the whole neighborhood. the reason they woke up because they heard a scream, an ear – piercing scream, a scream of terror, a horrifying scream, an afraid scream. It was sure that the scream was of the beggar because on the street where the beggar was walking he was no longer there . only his clothes were lying on the street.

CHAPTER TWO

Who could it be ?

Next morning everyone woke up and no one remembered anything. soon it was nightfall. some teenagers were having a party and soon the party was over and everyone then left. One girl named Amanda lived a little far away. So she got on her scooter and left. While she was driving

she passed an abandoned factory. Normally she would just ignore it. But today as soon as she passed the factory she heard some noises. She wondered "Who could be working at such a hour? Does someone need help "she thought.

she got down and made her way into the factory. As she was getting closer to the factory, the voice got louder and louder. As soon as she stepped into the factory the door behind her shut. She was trapped in there. She started screaming "let me out, let me out "but there was no one around. She thought that she should find another way out and started roaming in the factory. The factory was smelling terribly. And the voice was no longer heard. Soon it was morning. the girl never returned. her parents filed a report but none could find her. Now there were 2 missing people in the town including the beggar. And there was only 1 question in everyone's mind. ***Who Could It Be*** ?

CHAPTER THREE

James and David

After a long search by the police they eventually they found Amanda's clothes in the factory but her body was missing. So now it was understood that Amanda was dead. the police interrogated all the people who were in that party. finally, the police took 2 suspects. Their names were James and David. All the other people who were in the party said that James & David had a fight with Amanda. So the police took them in the custody. After a long interrogation they had the same answer that they didn't kill Amanda. So then the police went to James and David's parents they asked them what time did their kids come home, without any hesitation or showing any sign of suspicion they calmly replied "Around 11:30PM" and the people and the party said that everyone left around 11:15 so it was normal that they reach their homes by 11:30. Plus when the police took Amanda's and checked the handprints James and David's handprints weren't even there on amandas clothes. So the police were thinking that maybe they didn't really kill Amanda so then who did it. And even if they did kill Amanda then where would her body go and even if they would burn amandas body there was no sign of ash or any burning so after all these evidences even the police declared that James and David were innocent.

CHAPTER FOUR

One More Case

For Amandas case the police were still finding out who did it but until they could find out who did it one more case came up. There were 2 school boys. Both of them were best friends their names were Josh and William. Both of them were in the same school their summer holidays were going on. As they were very bored they thought of going camping Both of them packed their things and decided to meet under a big old banyan tree. Their mothers told both of them to reach home by 9 o' clock. Both of them thought that they would explore a cave so on their map they marked the cave as X. After hours of walking while trying to catch his breath Josh said exhausted "Are we there yet "While panting William said "Yeah just a little more ""You've been saying that from the past 3 hours "William really couldn't answer to that. Finally, at 8:30PM they could finally see the cave. They both were so happy that they did a little dance together. "Yeah woohoo finally we are here "said Josh "Yeah bro I told you so "said William excitedly. They quickly took their camera's and torch's out and went into the cave. They were so happy and excited that they forgot that they had to reach home by 9 o clock.

CHAPTER FIVE

Are we lost !

Both of them went into the cave the cave's entrance was bigger than two houses put on each other. "Dude this thing is huge "said William "It sure is "said Josh. As they were brave kids they were not scared of darkness and other things from which children are usually scared of. As they

went in they noticed something, that the cave was smelling terribly. It smelled like dead rat and eggs mixed together. Ignoring the smell, they walked on after 15minutes or so Josh asked William "U. hhhhh William are we lost "William confidently replied "No no not at all I know exactly where we are going ""Even I know where we are going! We are going straight ahead into a cave I am asking exactly where we are going said Josh irritated because I can't see the entrance of the cave through which we entered ". William turned around and saw that even he couldn't see the entrance. Everything was pitch dark. Then suddenly their torches started fluctuating and stopped working. It was so dark that they couldn't even see their own hand in front of their face. Josh stuttered William "W-W-Why did our torches stop working "William said "Don't worry I have an emergency light in my bag "then he removed it and switched it on. Then Josh said "Listen William I know you are very excited to explore this cave and want to explore more but now we are left with only an emergency light and I'm sure it's way past 9 o clock and our parents must be worried sick about us we should leave now ". Understanding the situation William agreed and replied "I understand Josh we can come another time and anyway it is just a normal cave, there's nothing special about it let's go ". Although they couldn't see the entrance they remembered through which way they came and started walking on.

CHAPTER SIX

Did You Hear That

Once they started walking they sort of remembered through which way they came. After walking Josh suddenly heard a low grrrr voice he turned back but couldn't see anyone. He asked William "Did you hear that noise ""Did you hear what "asked William "No nothing never mind "answered Josh. After 30 minutes or so they could finally see the entrance of the cave there was no bound to their happiness they ran toward she entrance. But then suddenly something grabbed William's leg and dragged him deep into the cave. He screamed "AHHHHHHH HELP ME I AM BEING DRAGGED BY SOMETHING "Josh ran to help but that something caught hold of him too but Josh was strong so he defended himself once and then accidently he stepped on the click button on the camera which was on the ground ignoring that Josh ran outside in full speed towards the entrance but that thing caught hold of him too and dragged him into the cave. The next morning when Josh and William didn't return Josh and William's parents filed a report to the police about the disappearance of their children. Even the police were worried all the people disappearing so they thought its time they call the higher ranks, the ones who are masters in solving any case the ones who are the legends of investigation the legendary team the **4 INVESTIGATORS**

CHAPTER SEVEN

4 Investigators

The 4 investigators were called. In case you didn't know 4 investigators were the team that could solve any mystery case. Their names were Bob, Harry , Miguel and Kenny. Once the 4 of them reached the police station, the police told them about the case and they immediately got to work. First they checked if there were any fingerprints on Amanda's, Josh's or William's clothes but they couldn't find any fingerprints so they wanted to move on to the next clue but they couldn't find any clue, then suddenly Harry's eyes went on the camera. He saw all the photos which were there in the camera but half of the photos were of the cave so now at least they knew where to find their next clue. Then in the photos something caught Harry's eyes it was a very dark picture but he could clearly see some green vines and he could see something at the back of the picture it was some kind of light but he just couldn't figure out what it was he asked others but even they couldn't figure out what it was. Bob said "Good at least now we will know where the find our next clue" Kenny said "Ok squad now we will meet here tomorrow at 9:00 clock and will head for the cave and bring everything you have to Miguel then reassuringly said to Josh and Williams parents who were crying miserably sitting in the corner of the room "Don't worry we will find out who did this to your children. You can count on us "saying this even Miguel left.

CHAPTER EIGHT

The Search Begins

Next morning everyone brought their supplies and met at the meeting point. Then everyone headed for the cave by 10:30 or 11:00 clock. Even though it was bright and sunny outside still it was dark inside the cave. The 4 investigators being brave and courageous weren't afraid very and had done this many times before. The 4 men headed inside the cave. As they didn't want to be lost in the big dark and long cave they kept really bright and big torches at every interval. After a while they started matching the photos on Josh's camera to their surroundings and all of them matched. They walked for hours together and finally they reached the end of the cave. They tried to find something that could give them a clue of what took Josh and William but they couldn't find anything it was just hard rock nothing else. "I guess somebody just kidnapped the kids and put the green vines for suspicion "said Kenny "I guess he is right" said Miguel "We should head back we are just wasting our time here ". Just as they were about to go Harry spotted a red light it was dim but it was visible "Hey hey guys wait can you see that light its just like the light we could see in the camera in one of the photos ""I think it's some kind of button try pressing it Harry "suggested Bob. As soon as he pressed the button a very bright light showed and no one could see anything and the whole cave disappeared.

What ! How did this happen ?

Suddenly everyone got up. Then Harry shrieked "What! Where are we! Where is the cave " . Around them there was no longer a cave it was a lab. Well it looked like a lab and there where guards everywhere. The 4 had no time to think they quickly hid behind a giant pillar. Miguel then said "The last thing I remember that Harry pressed some sort of button and then after that I just don't remember anything." I guess this must be some kind of secret door that led us here let's go check it out "suggested Kenny.

CHAPTER TEN

Why What When How ?

Slowly while avoiding the guards they started to look around the lab if they could find any clues. Surprisingly luck was with them. As soon as they went a little further they could see a scientist He was short and wore a typical white coat. They spotted something else also along with the scientist. "Hey aren't those Amanda, Josh and William and who are those other people "asked Miguel. They looked and saw their bodies which were inside a big glass tank. Each were in their own cylinder shaped glass tank. The tank was filled with some type of blue liquid and it looked like their bodies were preserved. All 4 of them were dumbfounded as they kept staring at the bodies. Then Kenny broke the silence and said "Ok so I have a lot of questions in my mind- first of all Why has he kept all these bodies in the tank, what does he plan to do with all of those bodies, how do we find out what he will do with the bodies and most of all just as he was about complete his sentence Harry interrupted him and said WHEN WILL WE SOLVE THE MYSTERY AND GET OUT OF HERE! "blurted Harry "Can't agree more with you but we have to find all those answers ourselves "said Bob then when he just finished his sentence the scientist barked commands to one of the guards "Hey you …. yeah you stay here and watch see that no one comes inside while I am inside ". Okay guys we have to sneak in and see what he is up to but we can't get caught "ordered Bob "Well don't you think we should just take the bodies and run. There's no point in searching and finding out it will only get us in trouble the other things are none of our business right thought aloud Harry "No what if he is more bodies and we have not even answered even one of the questions Kenny has asked and you know Kenny he isn't leaving this place without answering his questions asked right we have to solve this case after all we are not called the legendary 4 investigators for no reason , plus this is very fishy I have my suspicion on the scientist that he wants to meddle and create something with bodies . We have to solve this case and fast . So Harry you coming or not? said Bob "Ok fine "moaned Harry. "Ok so its decided we save Amanda, Josh, William and all of the other bodies and solve this mystery.

CHAPTER ELEVEN

The Stratergy

"But even if he has more bodies how do we save them "questioned Miguel "Good question but sadly I don't have the answer we'll figure that out when we do it "answered Bob. "Guys but first we have to find a safer spot to discuss out strategy "said Harry. They quickly found a big private plane and they had no idea what it was doing there but they just hid behind it. Ok my plan is that we just wait till nightfall we wait for the bodyguards to go to sleep and then we start our investigation and find out what he is up to "Bob said, Harry said "Yeah really good plan ok anyone any questions ""Nope "everyone said. "Ok then let the plan begin"

CHAPTER TWELVE

Plan In Action

Once nightfall occurred the 4 of them put their plan in Action. The 4 came out of their hiding place and then once they confirmed that the guards went to sleep. Then they reached into the room and opened the door and went inside. As soon as they entered they were shocked by what they saw they kept staring at the ghastly image in front of them. Thousands of bodies stored in the room all of them were in the same blue liquid in which Josh, William, Amanda were kept. They just couldn't imagine. So many questions came in their minds like what were so many bodies doing here? How did they come here? Why did the scientist want so many bodies.? "Hey guys did you all notice something said Miguel "What "asked everyone "They all are wearing one type of cloth it's like the clothes that you wear in a hospital .The shirt was a light blue color and it had dark blue stripes and same with the pajama's ""Yeah dude I wonder why but "asked Bob "I think the scientist is experimenting on them " answered Kenny

The Truth

Then suddenly they heard footsteps and quickly hid behind a table. The scientist was talking to himself saying "Yes tonight I will rule the whole world. Exactly today at midnight the power will be all mine ha ha ha ha ha ha ha ha "."What power is he talking about ,what ruling the world is he "thought Miguel "Something fishy is going on and we haven't even figured out what he will do the bodies "said Bob.

Then the scientist went inside deep into the room "We need to follow him and find out what is he up to "said Kenny and everybody agreed. Everyone slowly crept behind him and started to follow him. They tried to keep up with him but lost his trail. There were just too many rooms they couldn't keep track. Instead they entered a different room in the center of the room there was a big board and something was drawn on it. At first they couldn't understand what it was but then they found out that was a diagram. In it few figures of some bodies were drawn After looking and understanding the diagram Bob finally explained that "First some tubes are connected to a tank and all the tubes which were connected to the tank again extend from the other side and are connected to a big tub which looks like a giant cauldron. All the tubes which are connected to the cauldron then extend from the other side of the cauldron which are all connected to a giant robot ." " Okay now I understand that first the scientist drains out the energy from the human bodies then in that big cauldron the energy is converted into electricity and then it is supplied to the giant robot, this is how the giant robot functions. With that robot he plans to take on the world" finished Kenny . " This is 1 big case "sighed Miguel . We have to do so much in so little time. I don't even feel like doing this " . "We have to do this mission we promised Amanda's ,Josh's ,and William's parents right "said Bob.

CHAPTER FOURTEEN

A Giant Giant Robot

"Guys quick the scientist is heading this way we have to get out of here " warned Harry who was guarding the door. "Let's go search into the other rooms maybe we can find something more useful "suggested Kenny. They quickly ran into an another room before the scientist could come. The room they ran into was very big. As soon as they went in the room they stared aghast at the image in front of them. They were shocked, dumbfounded and kept staring. In front of them was a giant, giant, giant robot and didn't look anything like a regular one. It had inbuilt weapons a three layers' protection shield and was as big as a 20 story building. "If he is planning to take over the world with that this thing maybe he can I guess "said Harry who was astonished by the size of the robot . "Shut up Harry nothing is going to happen by thinking negative "scolded Kenny "What I'm just thinking "protested Harry "Enough fighting you both "scolded Bob "I guess there must be some kind of switch or button to shut off the electric supply ""Nope no such switch "said Miguel "While you people were talking I searched the whole room ". All 4 of them were in a fix. They had to find the switch, they had to save the bodies, they also had to take care that none watches them, and there were just too many rooms. "Well let's start searching shall we, nothing is going to happen just by worrying "said Bob trying to encourage everyone

Room To Room

In the first few rooms nothing useful was found. in one room there were potions. As soon as Miguel saw the potions he exclaimed "Ooh this sure looks interesting! look at those different, colorful, exciting, exotic, bubbling, blissful, marvelous, tempting, terrific, playful, chemicals. They are waiting to be experimented the urge of the chemicals is very tempting. You know when I was in school I used to get full marks in chemistry I was the class topper or maybe you can say the school topper. So listen why don't you people go on and keep searching the rooms I will stay here and make a potion that will stop the robot from working ""Ok fine with us everyone agreed ""Yay" said Miguel who was acting like a five-year-old baby who just got a free supply of ice-cream forever then he went hopping into the room. "Ok now even if we don't find the switch at least we have our class topper to rely on "chuckled Kenny. "Ok come on guys we have to find the switch before midnight. We don't have much time left "said Bob in a serious voice. In the first 5 rooms there was nothing but in the next 5 rooms there was metal junk then looking further the next 5 rooms were used as storage rooms. In the next room there were two big fridges "This guy sure has a big appetite "thought Harry to himself. Then in the next room there were gaming laptops Ps4, Xbox everything a kid would ever want. "He is an adult but he still plays video games "thought Bob to himself. Then in the next room there was a mini theater, in the next room there was a big library filled with books "Well at least he reads something that is not childish "thought Kenny to himself. Then with the next 10 rooms combined there was the scientist's room. As they entered the room they were amazed the scientist had a huge mega triple size TV, a big Jacuzzi, an extra big size fridge filled with cakes, pizzas and pastries. The 3 helped themselves thoroughly. Harry who was enjoying himself totally forgot about the case and he pressed the button of the TV remote and out of nowhere a vault appreared who became a little scared by the sudden appearance of the vault "OOOPS "said Harry "What did you do now Harry "said Bob in an irritated voice "I pressed the button of the TV remote I thought some TV would help ""Oh how could you even think of TV in such a time "

CHAPTER SIXTEEN

What's the Password ?

"Look what you have done Harry. We can't even reach to Miguel now "said Bob who was frustrated "Sorry "said Harry who was ashamed of himself. Then Bob screamed and irritated he punched the vault then suddenly a robotic voice said **Access not granted need password** " Did the vault just say that " asked Harry " Yes the vault said it " said Kenny who was sitting on a sofa " I guess this is the vault that leads us to the switch that is why it is in the scientists room and it is so highly protected " The door said that access not granted so there must be some password just think If I were a scientist what password would I have kept " " You guys have been thinking the password from the past 10 minutes we don't have much time for this " groaned Kenny " Yeah and you are not helping " said Bob " Harry get up screamed Bob and stop eating ,help us in guessing the password of this . " Harry who had helped himself with the 8th piece of pastry belched loudly and said " Ok I guess I'll help you maybe it can be god of the world or king of the world " before he could say a word after that the vault said **" Access granted "** . "Yes you did it said Bob "You did it Harry you guessed the password ". Then the 3 of them went inside. Then after walking a few steps they found a big switch all of them put all their might and put off the switch. "Yes we finally did it "cheered Harry "No Harry our main mission is not over yet we have to save all those bodies "said Kenny "Yeah sorry I totally forgot about it "said Harry " What else could you expect from Harry "mumbled Bob under his breath .

CHAPTER SEVENTEEN

The Antidode

"Come on quickly we have to find Miguel and tell him about this "said Kenny "Yeah let's go "said Harry. They quickly ran and reached in the potions room " Miguel " screamed Harry " Hi guys so did you find the switch " asked Miguel " Tell you what surprisingly we did find it " said Harry joyfully " Well that's good news and I have some good news on my side too I saw the chemical that was used in the tanks to preserve the bodies and I found an antidote that can give all the people their energy back they just have to have a teeny tiny bit of it and, boom back to normal " said Miguel who was feeling very proud of himself " Ok guys now we don't have to stay here for a long time we will give this antidote to every person who is kept in the tank and now let's go from here . We don't want the scientist to see us lurking around here, Do we ? "said Bob. Then when they saw the first person they removed the tube and pulled the person out and as they were about to give the antidote to that person they heard a shout "Hey who are you???? What are you doing here? How did you come in? Guards Guards!! Come get these intruders "screamed the scientist! Before the guards could come Bob told Miguel "Miguel you go with the antidote and give it to each and every person you see, we will take care of the guards "At first Miguel was hesitant and refused but then he agreed and then slowly slipped out without the scientist noticing. Then when the guards came Bob, Harry and Kenny fought with them at first they were winning but then more and more guards kept coming "This is taking forever the guards are not ending they just keep coming. What shall we do "said Harry while panting. "Yeah I agree with Harry this is not stopping "said Kenny. Then Bob said "Ok we will stall them and give some time to Miguel until can give the antidote to everyone ". Then it was like cats chasing mice they ran and ran. Meanwhile Miguel had given the antidote to everyone then he told everyone "Come on guys we have to help my friends "the scientist had so many bodies stored so of course the guards were outnumbered they ran for their lives and hid in a room timidly.

Trump Card

No that was my research for years you destroyed everything. I will not leave you "screamed the scientist in agony. Then the scientist put on a jetpack which was attached to his shoes "Well now it is time to show you my trump card saying that flew where the giant, giant, giant robot was kept while he was away Kenny said "Well let's see how his trump card works "everyone chuckled. Then they heard heavy footsteps it was the giant, giant, giant robot "Then Harry acted as if he was very scared he screamed "AHHHH Oh No it is such a giant robot he is going to crush us help me "said Harry in sarcasm "Yeah that's right I am going to crush you "cackled the scientist. Then as soon as he was about to load his weapons and started to shoot everyone the robot suddenly stopped. "Why did this stop. Start you piece of metal junk " The scientist started banging it. "Well I guess some people put off the switch which was in the room "mocked Kenny. "What! when did you put off the switch and how did you know about it "screamed the scientist. "Well no point in screaming now you are coming with us to the custody "Kenny. "Noo" wailed the scientist . " You have ruined years of my experiment I will not spare you "

CHAPTER NINETEEN

Back Home

Then all the 4 went from where they came in the lab they pressed the same red button and Boom they were back in the same old cave. "It feels like we were in the lab for days and days "said Miguel. Then all of them went out of the cave and went into the police custody Josh, William and Amanda were sent to their parents and all the other people were also sent to their own homes. "Well it's about time we also went back to our own homes "said Bob "Yeah you're right this was a really long mission but it was fun "chuckled Harry. "No not at all nobody is going home without a party. We really do deserve it "exclaimed Miguel. "Can't agree more with you Miguel "said Kenny. If you insist said "Bob and Harry ".